W9-ABZ-443

Song of the Cicadas

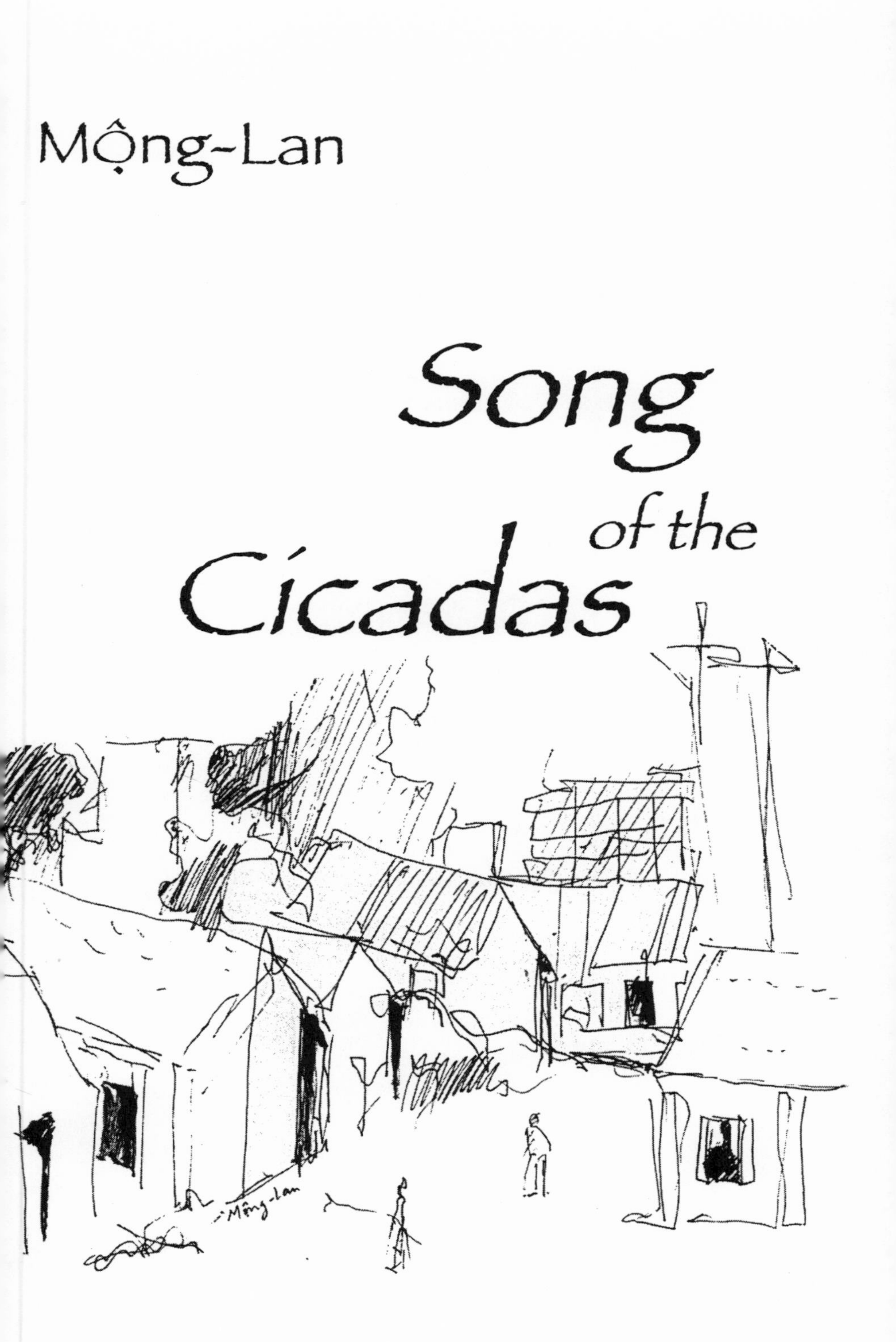
Mộng-Lan
Song of the Cicadas
Mộng-Lan

Printed in the United States of America

LC 00-054391
ISBN 1-55849-307-7

Designed by Sally Nichols
Set in VN Tien Giang
Printed and bound by Sheridan Books, Inc.

Library of Congress Cataloging-in-Publication Data

Mộng-Lan, 1970–
Song of the cicadas / Mộng-Lan.
p. cm.
ISBN 1-55849-307-7 (pbk. : alk. paper)
1. Vietnamese Americans—Poetry. 2. San Francisco (Calif.)—Poetry.
3. Vietnam—Poetry. I. Title.
PS3613.O64 S65 2001
811′.6—dc21 00-054391

British Library Cataloguing in Publication data are available.

For . . . the keepers of this book

Contents

Acknowledgments

To the following journals and anthologies where these poems first appeared, and to my editors, my thanks and appreciation:

Five Fingers Review: "Letters"; "A New Việt Nam"
Fourteen Hills: "Gravity"
The Iowa Review: "Things Human"
The Kenyon Review: "Field"; "Grotto"; "Ravine"
Luna: "Lake"; "Train"
Making More Waves: New Writing by Asian American Women (Boston: Beacon Press, 1997): a slightly different version of "Silence of Form"
Manoa: A Pacific Journal of International Writing: "the taste"
Pleiades: "Hunger"; "Song of the Cicadas"; "Twilight"
The Pushcart Prize Anthology XXIV: "Sand, Flies & Fish" (reprint)
Quarterly West: "Sand, Flies & Fish"
The Vietnam Review: a slightly different version of "Sounding Sa Đéc"
Watermark: Vietnamese American Poetry & Prose (New York: Asian American Writers' Workshop, 1998): slightly different versions of "The Long Biên Bridge," "The Golden Gate Bridge," and "Sounding Sa Đéc"

I would like to thank the judges of the Juniper Prize for selecting my manuscript.

To my family for their love and support, I express gratitude. To Jane, hearty thanks for guidance and friendship. To my dear friends, appreciation and affection.

1

Grotto

Vịnh Hạ Long (Bay of the Landing Dragon), Tonkin Gulf

1

The rower   gaunt as his oar
lets us out   conscious
of not getting his 5,000 đồng
he stands ankles in cool water
holding onto the state-owned boat
for support   his skin the same color
as the mud   my eyes follow
the morning tides ebbing
from the dock
(flash of residue
undulating)   turquoise solid
as the mountains   mold has blackened
the boat's belly
lapping at it
clear water runs over sky

grotto of swimming bats   I do not swallow
the darkness   rocks under my feet
are piranhas' mouths if I miss a step

stalagmite meeting stalactites   coincidences
taking forever to form

2

the eclipse's purple cast
throws everyone
off balance
inside she clutches onto the image
of her lover in case she falls
her body a black and white lily
against the gorge
of sky this morning she ate nothing
but a banana to quell
her upset stomach
a well drips its musical water
in the back rock kings play chess
a centuries-old tournament
neither wins

dusky unbirth of pre-memory
she forgets to bring a flashlight
to disarm the rocks stalagmites
a line of prayer to hook
her thoughts

3

bats swallow my shadow
when the ocean swallows us
from these pages what will the sky speak
of the bat grottos?
twenty years the ugliness
forgotten

back to port: bone sky
mist bleeds over the mountain ridges
over water barges snailing

racket of diesel motors
a huge stone head
imagining us
two rocks two cocks fighting
a vigilant rock dog stares in silence

my hand on the horizon
of its tail the scaly sieve

The Long Biên Bridge

1

Seeing the Long Biên Bridge
on a pastel
map of Hà Nội its image
one-dimensional and slumberous an undug
grave
I would never have guessed
it for what it really is: a patchwork of engravings
love-entwined names (skin of words
the unstripping instants of flesh)

graffiti mostly "*Cấm Đái!*" (No Urinating!)
altered
from bombings shell-shocked doctored countless times

was it the architect Eiffel
who drew this bridge into reality?
its black strokes hanging over the sky
like a leg of the Eiffel Tower
placed across two shores

2

the Red River
stripping silt   shale
over crimson shores fluxes
urgent   snail-patient   penitent

the rains
bloat it white and phantasmic
at its banks
she launders the family clothes
next to where the buffalo shits
where her children
shit   rings around her swollen ankles

children play mindlessly in satellite
shores loaded with strange
luster
that body of dazzling light

3

she's learned how to talk back
without talking
she's learned how to defend herself
in her small way

her older sister
who refuses to marry him
sits near the bridge amassing
vegetables for sale
mounds of mint
hills of water spinach
guavas   bananas "the poor man's fruit"
swords of sugarcane
flopping scales like huge tongues
ready to weigh

discreet as pickpockets
peril waits
between rusty spokes
underneath
spinning bike tires   but

motion saves the day

4

not having to think
of motion
the villagers commuting from the countryside
to the city pedal
no thought but to force the legs the foot
the hands from swerving
head straight
not really looking at anything   but the whole

in sync
they know not to hold their breaths

the wind moves through you in conditional
tense of spokes   tattered clothes
conical straw hats

friction of atmospheres
flapping clothes hinting the body's
bony outline
hair that knows itself through wind

5

acidic arcs
urine stains   tumbling rain

the bridge shudders from the history
it knows

peasant-fighters   rumbling feet   bodies
dragged over its steel ribs
throaty cries like rusty parts
toe caught   tire thong lost

still the urgency   the pedaling

6

rustic bodies
with the weight of the day's work
splayed over trailing shadows

bodies illuminated like insomniac
thought
pealing from one outline to another
the endless chase

encaged chickens
whiz by   chickenfeathers
strip the sky of wait
and water water

you know not to hold your breath
wind-intoxicated
waiting for *it*
the minute it comes you want
to escape

Lake

1

not in cramped houses
with censorious walls
but in anonymous air
the lake's mist shields
them from comment
one gesture kindling
another that's how I espy
them the lovers
hand sparked on the hip
serpentine hair
draped along the body

no matter that the rats scuttle
like shuttlecocks
around the lake's lips drinking
in the lovers' discourse
their embrace makes sure
the world doesn't exist
subject of noise
the winter day's pantomime

2

moving in two worlds
the tortoises   the swallows
their minds
the elderly practice Tai Chi
at 6 in the morning
around the lake
one gesture flows into another
arms to wind
heel to ground
sure the world does exist
the matter of their bodies
not their mist

shrugging sleep off morning's shoulders
the tofu lady sings
the morning is a burning
kettle of thuốc bắc   Chinese herbs
my aunt's roosters croon the battlewire cage
their kept secrets
wanting death is wanting nothing

3

raging under phố

the kerosene fire

a cigarette fizzing a female hand

the insouciant days   quiet burning like writing

clash of shadows

feet adrift

4

rats leap

for food-scraps around the lake

the northeasterly wind casts its spells

ashes of money burnt at an offering

purling incense

faraway the shade of dried squid

burning   children have their butts up in gutters

the fierce motorcycled streets

at the juncture

where matter dreams

& pantomimes begin to speak

you gather from its incandescence

your world

Ravine

as they come
through the endless branchings of rooms
after bronze Chinese coins are cast
strange heat of silences
you stand doused in sleep

the back of your neck
is a bird's shadow ascending
your spine a line
a ravine where things are lost:
marbles the sound of a cello
faded photos brittle letters
I lace your body with my hands
your legs loaves of bread
your feet slippery fish
broken fins
swimming through uncharted waters

under your right shoulder blade
I find something shiny black
a new revolver

as they come for you
I wipe sleep off your shoulders
put the gun in your hands
tell you to aim
you point
to your head

Field

Crows land like horses' neighs
rush of rocks

how many buffalo
does it take to plow a disaster?
how many women to clean
up the mess?

shoots of incense
hotly in her hands
she bows toward the tombstones
face of her son
how many revolutions for us to realize?

her windless gray hair
becomes her   she knows this
there is no reason
to dye what she's earned

rain quiet as wings
on her back

A New Việt Nam

1

sweat of bolts & nails
muscle like steel & metal

architects work at a ripping pitch
pounding out a new capitol

around the lakes
morning to evening the ground explodes
liquid concrete
mercury ambling down streets

you think you are the noise

men pick at French-laid concrete like crows

shovels and picks at shoulders
they stand knees in earth

pain trots down the street

how life would've been more than noise

how events should've happened

2

Huế — what do you make of chance
life's but a dollar a day

what should you say when a person
dies each day in the Demilitarized Zone scrounging for scrap metal
shrapnel unexploded
bullets & bombs on trays like shrimp
before tourists?

the hills now there now disappearing
white claws stream down from dumped chemicals
a fun house of horror

still after decades the Khe Sanh Combat Base
is nearly flat; the Hồ Chí Minh trail winds
thirty minutes to Laos & National Highway 1 threading
the country in one

is it chance that the Huế dialect is a giddy
fish never to be hooked?

the language is imagined by the land's vapors
fluctuating hills
the mirage of white sand
by dreams of the brood
of cows walking through white mountains

a woman fries her smoky meal
next to a moon crater

3

honey-moon light swoops over the valleys
upon the Đà Lạt mountains
like squadrons
a man buys two bunches of bananas in half a second

I linger & face the remark
of the vendor *"chúi nào cũng như vậy hết*
cô hiền quá đi vào buôn bán đi"
("the bananas are all the same you're too naive go into business")

I pass the Nuclear Research Center
prop from an old movie
on a deserted mountain

toward the Domaine de Marie Convent a pink
church "once house to 300 nuns" someone waves

then past the cemetery a mountain of crosses
which doesn't stop rising

2

Sand, Flies & Fish

1

I take a glass of the expiring sun, sipping it. Cambodia's terse mountains to my right. the Gulf of Thailand in front of me. the border police in their rumpled uniforms are still as backdrop characters. the hot sun mats their hair down in neat sweat lines. a white gull pecks at black sand. the sand is so black you think you're close to hell. I wait for the sun to come down on the sea. nausea for it. in the evenings the national Vietnamese news blares from loudspeakers. world's slow motions. fires' haze. sky's blood draining over boneless ocean.

2

even if I described detail by detail to you, the
whole would escape you. how can you see
the southern edge of the continent— what would
that matter? or the black sand grading into the
blueness of the sea, or the vigilant Cambodian
mountains. what would it matter if I told you
ships dock in front of my window. that when not
in my room, I wander through villages eating
dirt, whatever I can beg. it happens to a woman.
these things happen. these accidents. I watch
my stomach bloat with the seed of a man who
was a shadow. I pick at the salt crop gleaming
in evening light, and steal whatever I can to sell
in the markets. the land's lungs are strong. it fills
my baby's ears with its tenor.

3

this edge of the world is a knife. the motorcycle
taxi drivers wait humped, clocks on the dock, that
dulled look for a customer. everything an
illusion of another.

4

salt fields glisten from ocean light. there is so much light here you could die from it. bamboo houses stilted on black sand. houses so close they share the same reflection on the water. pepper fields like black eggs dry in the sun. here I became pregnant and had my first child. his fingers learned to quicken at the touch of sand. he let fish swim in and out of his lungs and bloodstream. the ocean and sky, one medium to him, he walked in both. one day I let him go too far, and the black waves came down and took him.

5

fishermen, rapt in another world. their harvest
dries on large metal nets laid aslant — dust settles
on the squid's splayed arms. squatting, smoking,
noticing every ripple on the road. their skins
sinewy, pasty as clay. lying on hammocks,
crowns of mosquitoes and flies over their heads.
they know your real name without asking.

6

her rat's nest hair. she peels it from her face. the children pound her with fists. she sweeps her cane, left and right, screaming something. the children laugh. hysteria in her eyes. bobbing up and down, she slaps down money at a cafe stand to buy food. they laugh. in a tremor she throws the food at the crowd. they laugh again. her clothes are ragged, shirt torn at the seams, her skirt dusty, feet thick and calloused. more fists at her. jab of her cane. a man scoops the children away from her. clasping the seams of the crowd, she exhales orange and white fire. eyes pierce her back. in her drunken momentum she crosses the floating bridge without paying toll. sulfur frothing down her chin, her rat's nest hair blazes to the skies.

7

they watch the land, watch the air. the dust gathering. strips of white ghost-cloth tied across their foreheads. the grey-haired, heads down, talking. the young with round eyes full of fruit, rice, cradles of incense, yellowing black & white photos of grandparents, great-grandparents. they dress him up, the resemblance of him. powdered, rouged, his hair combed back. what he was in life, more so in death. my baby died a quiet death. except for the birds, there was no one to witness.

8

the ocean curves around the land like a fish
caught on a hook, murmuring something to itself.
bodies crooning. stark bamboo houses. women
beat shrimp into dust, after they're laid out in
perfect pink squares to dry. bowels unload,
unweave into the Gulf of Thailand.

9

pigs arrive at the dock each morning squealing
for their lives. rows of squid drying on nets like
ghosts. the whole village is well preserved
smelling of dried fish and squid. Vietnamese
boys watch Cambodian TV. the black sand wet
under my feet speaks too in another language,
teeth chafing against teeth dialect against dialect,
tongue buckling north and south into coast and
soil. what country is this? it used to be my
home, where my child was born, where he died.
it was probably best that all he saw was this sun.

3

Trajectory

1

in this art
you may liken me to a line
of simple deliberate strokes
"a curve
that a body
describes in space"

2

San Francisco you called
my city by the sea its pastel appeal
loaded with languid
charms though yesterday I walked again through
the same place that we passed   the site
of a chisel-stabbing   a shrine of
shining candles & callas
was built for the martyr who tried to break
up the mugging
not the scene it used to be

3

it used to be
you thought the hallucinatory
ability was a "superior
development of the ability
to imagine" & I imagined
you hallucinating your adolescent
days & nights away
as you must do now
with your roommate fat with your books
she splits their spines
leaving large coffee-stained eyes
to spy on you in your precious moments
alone to tell us about the writing
of which you never talk
the hidden anvils being struck
with each oblique thought
you scour away scars
traumatic dialogues of which you were a part

smalltalk like clawing hydrogen
cold corridors
earthquake dolor in Los Angeles
your students' disinterest

4

but death you won't invite
your life's trajectory
will tail infinity's clear line

dreaming the same dream one night
we will speak
of the poem
that has never been written

for Vidhu

The Golden Gate Bridge

1

the wind's moods & resolutions
erase tendrils
that grow
from the sea (to engrave around *it*
have that as a dish
you could eat)

your fully fed body thrashing
in the Atlantic
was found near the Golden Gate Bridge
no one understands

the un-life the mis-life
propelled you

had you known
the best thing in the world
to be is struggling

2

there are few bicyclists
here the ones who brave
the adamant wind
are helmeted professionals or stern amateurs

cars dominate swerve
over earth's contours

I pull up your body
breathe
my breath
into you & we walk as far
West as the continent allows

your words fill
millennium of
odd waters

3

Magritte rocks
shrouded in fog

rough hewn hands rose tinctured
skin bared & sunburnt
pavement under feet
gravelward runs to sea   a flag white
at infinity

above the bridge
the universe of red rust

thicker than wrists metal cords
pass us   lax or hasty as the years
yearly repainted

4

at a place of no memory
a moment

hands feet
caught
on cord
wheels drive over & around a distinct view
is whirled into a configuration matter never slowing
engraved into air

(machines
drive off
the sea eats

ground?

shake

sufficient
to change
currents)

5

suspension of cold breaths

one rock two
mist

a fallen hand house down below entranced
in foam and waves
its foundation red walls lined roof

dust framed in body's image
eyes blown truant
with hair

San Francisco of paved feet
seaward runs
the mind projects us forward

the body
holds us back

6

a door appears   a tomb

stoic   a metal door bounded by stone
time-occluded
door that would endure unopened

on the bridge that suspends

the idea
of the person who walks
on it

instants

Silence of Form

1

The wind has everything to do with this city
this bridge   this time
these rocks this place
ravaged divested
of human form
the fire creating this lesion
charred wood   trunks thinned ashen

the wind sculpts soil
into bodies that walk in the realm
of dreams
it angers the sea
pulling its threads shifting the drowned
knotted tendons   false teeth rotten
& roaming tongues
spitting out quick bodies
shiny black backs & blind feet

fog walks around the ocean
as surf swell & mist deafen

2

one shore two shores overlapping
like long necks   long thighs or
the form of sex
mist of forearms
hands floating
fingers unsure of physical matter
death swooping but ignored
uvular angular limbs
(hair caught in mouth cheek against stomach)
uteral elliptical a mango carved
slippery as seaweed
treading skin in the dark to watery rhythms
of the salsa & it keeps on raining
& it doesn't matter
that the idle women next door are looking
in through the sweat & it doesn't matter
that sweat pours like rain
tasting of the sea
& sometimes it doesn't
matter there isn't love

3

you there the woman
who tries not to be violated

"sangra
pero functiona"
so he says the ugly condomless thing
what is one to do with it
you ask what is one to do
with it?

he walks toward window
jumps onto roof urinates
into bushes

comes back
carrying the night's nakedness
a black
cold to touch
Guanajuato's 3 A.M. mountain-murmuring
in his eyes
the town's echo
of solitary lights
under nails the coyotes' howl

4

the boy who hung himself
was a mandolin player
& that was all surviving
only his twenty-second birthday

they say that he loved
to play the mandolin daily
& that was all

olive skinned he played as no one
should've

& hung
himself that was it

5

what do people hear
when they see you?

6

the phosphorescence of the sea
has a cello's resonance
dusk curves
over clouds of silver stones cast
an augury overlooked
la luna llena brushes thatched roofs
& sand bodies love-entwined
the persistent chant of salty foam
satin wind
& coral waters gouge deep
lines into border rocks

sea anemones
mimicry of fish
gush of snails cling for their lives
along the coast unwashed underarm matter
tide pools wait
for the stone-eating sea

I have a dream
of you
diving against pastel skies
pear-perfect
smooth as a well-oiled crane
(as when you nude arise from slumber
in a centrifugal swing
legs tucked toes pointed
pulling you forward)
tense then relaxed
hands dipping to toes
your body opening out
a pocketknife
falling

we are at the edge where ocean
laps land
on cliff a silver house as if painted

I imagine you posing for me
arms outstretched ready to plunge
into another dimension
camera in hand I ask nothing
of you I take only this
picture of hesitation
silence of horizon & rocks

7

asleep your breathing cut short
then released controls the room's movements
metal chair wicker basket made in Mexico
your socks September slant
of light thrown against walls

leaving tomorrow
not telling
words no longer contain
your blood refuses
nocturnal hand still as ash

clothes strewn
on floor two-day old banana peel
breathing prolonged cut short

8

skin & odorous flesh
body that fails in time
hands dried by salt that have worked the sea
hands unknown
to the sea madness-soused hands

death was here unnoticed
swelling breaking brewing
birds glassy & black

waves worming
silver stones stuck in sky
sand born breathless

the taste

of a sonata adrift
your blanket the moon the sun
through trees specks of pepper
night wobbles a drunkard
at the dialectal borders
something is happening in the world explosions
firecrackers in night sky
like the coral's patient act
you untangle yourself from the net
of a dream
love was something you invented
drawing your shadows on rock

Song of the Cicadas

1

knowing hunger
the fool doesn't starve
plans fall apart
like playing-card skyscrapers
to want of nothing that's the rule of Buddhists
you say it is fate perhaps
that it should've been then not before or after
we meet when we think drink of each other
of the ocean the rains
trains corrugate the day unwittingly
my hand writes
pigeons coo like bedsprings of lovers
someone keeps opening the windows
the doors

2

the doors
open to tunnels we're crawling
time-shoveling in some foreign land
I learn to listen
your words   meaning
the moment I meet you at the airport
the hundredth time   in my sleep
I've met you
breathing in the you that isn't
from the Bay the ocean seen is as ample
cicadas drone
their dear songs braced in a fever
it usually happens
after the end begins

3

after the end begins
patience takes us
eyes salmon-flattened
fish through these pages
I slit my life in half   out gushes white music
impulsive acts   I wake up   another day living
with eyes closed   revised   veneer of calm
a passionate person
and a companion are two different things   at least
you have a romance   nothing to lose
I have my sanity
of which the lights are turned on   off
a pantomime where nothing needs to be said
thinking I'm dead so I don't really die

4

thinking I'm dead so I don't really die
(with thought
time stretches shrinks)
in this invented love
I drag my body snakeskin from here to there
fall to sleep hoping the mattress is your body
the pillow your face
that you might taste my skin
glimpse your dreams
then I wake up cold
you are nowhere near
but in my lungs ripped out rushing for air
must I stop this voice
is this voice the land's?

5

is this voice the land's?

transformed into art

keeping the world in motion

not noticed but when missing

ask when the two

of us will meet

were we made for this?

clay bodies vulnerable

prone

to delusions

the stone moves

from magnetic impulses

exhilarated flows

lost in your neck thighs your

6

lost in your neck thighs your
body a hardy root in midwinter terse
nothing unnecessary threshed into poem
imprint of your hand on my hips
your voice trapped
in my nervous system
the Spring awakens
mistakenly
your experiences absorbed in me
here are my lungs
singed with night wasp-wings for lips
black-red beetles
for eyes candle stubs for toes
hands white as sheets

7

hands white as sheets
skin subtle as persimmons
where the skin breaks at the fullest
curve the milk of your breath
flows down to grasp the bottom
for once not cynical or quick
but the slide long and silky
unlived life
your breath is red yet cool
to the mouth
a landscape of matches
cigarette butts ashes
stammering our tongues
knowing hunger

Hunger

chocolate breeze of Calle Mina:
Oaxaca village of scorpions
saintly mauves & hollows

backs to brick walls church crevices
pressed groins
there's the purged odor of men & women
in wasp-infested rooms
listen to the cry

cerveza spins the air
into a whir of bronzed flesh
the *Zócalo* is washed a veneer of stories guitar strums
the hundred year old oak
showers moon-coins
on red tile

society keeps you alive where anything
could happen
the heat hustle of rug vendors
comply with no one
the shadows
nor the dire air

Twilight

1

she drags her gangrened foot two miles back
over the loam pass
of the Palenque jungle

monkeys howl the illogical twilight
fireflies bloom around *la gordita*
a succulent vision

toads' tongues click
a leaf drifts & lands

the path is empty a truck passes
he talks of guns & tequila
burning his stomach

of the man who sells his wife
for tequila & *pistolas*

2

three hammocks down
a man tattooed from neck to foot
his mushroom body
sleeps as if dead
at times somnambulates   joints answering
widowed steps

I wake up like the tattooed man
dreaming of another's life
whisk off the scorpion
crossing the bend
of my elbow

a thud a click
the expiring fire beyond arm's length

I rise to walk in the wilderness
of the monkeys' rant

Things Human

1

he collects human teeth and bones
nails and hair
anything left over
that tells of a person

his companions
cut rounded smoothened filed down
he goes into the fields of nails
and hair
never finding his way out

2

the body clean
supple
grime rubbed
off until her thighs were raw

her legs hung by ankles
upside down like pants left to dry
anchored by the men's laugher
licking her   like candy
stones on the ground   eyes

3

how I've come to this place
no one knows
conversations I hear like silence
only worse

in the jar mountain air
hermetically sealed
packets of stars
desiccated   waiting for water

4

Sounding Sa Đéc

The world was huge and complex yet very clear.
—Marguerite Duras

Shock of body against shock of land and sea—
I've traveled to Sa Đéc to find you
I've airplaned across the huge and clear Pacific
stretching imaginary like mathematics
I've many times ferried across the Mekong
an onerous expanse of oblivion and poverty
and listened to it
and wept—
I find the primary school soybean-gold with lucid blue trimmings
where your mother taught
and today school is letting out early for a patriotic
holiday: hordes of mothers and fathers
perched intent
on their seats to motorcycle their children home—they could be waiting
waiting waiting
for Christ or the Buddha himself
to materialize
from dust

when I see a Chinese-styled mansion from afar ornate
with painted storytelling tiles I think
this must have been an important place
and it still is the government has transformed it into
a police station you can see four or five policemen
with their feet propped up on the table playing cards
my guide tells me this was where *the lover* lived
and this the lover's father's palace (he was the mandarin of Sa Đéc)
I don't know if I should believe her though the palace (not *blue* blue)
is facing the Mekong and under the police station sign
they've another prohibiting photos

as luck would have it (or sheer will)
I see your ghost as a child
in a simple white dress walking
by that house next to that familiar branch of the Mekong
and I can hear your high heels clacking
stares trailing behind you like clanking cans

in Vĩnh Long I see you sipping jasmine tea
next to the silvery Mekong
a nova slides down the whispering sky
slipping into the Mekong like an oar
all this a precursor
to your drunken stupor later in life?

Sa Đéc dusty provincial town in the South
a town like the others but here every cell
of my body is tracing your past
(where Indochina's mist has fashioned you bird-boned
North America's dreams
have steeped my marrow with thickness)
your childhood movements emblazoned in shift
of air guide me
marrow in my body
to stillness of song
rapture of humble people rupture of proud lives
in everything

that tells of the past   your past   our present:
rank bickering marketplaces
rusty ferries with their thunderous prewar motor
brick factories like large domed ant hills
where inside adolescent girls dig into earth
clay gloves up to their chins
sun-wizened men and women watching
the spirit of the old Mekong
unchanged   unchanging

one month later in Hà Nội I hear on the
Vietnamese national news that you've passed
away in France and your complex
life
in a syncopated   instant
tangos before me

Train

1

the train snakes Sài Gòn-south
groping to his seat
he nearly trips over the villagers
the twenty-pound bag
of jasmine rice
conversation
of the Frenchman the German
speaking in abrupt English
(lives enamored of movement)

the woman looks
to her breast suckled
the baby bundled in burps & hand-me-downs

you don't notice him
his back arching arms shaking
between flapping door of washroom
you don't hear the acidic arc

2

you are in the loud tunnel between Huế and Đà Nẵng
down below   ocean

you don't notice the woman
her miscarriage
she had thrown the fetus on the ancestral grounds
handed it to the gods
as a sacrifice
her tooth a die
rolling on the tile floor
from his blow
all over her back   red embroidery

notice her eyes

Letters

She has become like her mother
her insides blooming
she calms the gusts of hands & feet
heartbeats delicate as geranium buds

he's the salve of her sleep
writing her letters over eleven years
before the rats nibble on them
the house reads the words of his delirium
which keeps the beams from rotting
the cracks from spreading paint from fading
blanketing sun & moon the mist
grays the decade

at times he shakes from malaria
forehead feverish ice in his bones
salve of his
disease she's eleven years away

her one eye
observes the grapefruit rinds worming
on the dirt
a love letter seen askew
divides the days of mist
the house too having read
them is preserved

Gravity

in memory of my aunt

1

Spring & timbre
of my own rhythms wild in grief
she eats rice mangoes
with shrill fingers
I hold the chopsticks between my hands
watch her eat & think of the dry season
The silence between us brims
but for the gestures
the footsteps veering
away her voice chiding the grandchild
who crawls into her lap
the head a fallen fruit

Tree of her back
bent by a constant wind

2

What I witness is written in the lines of my hands
the dead don't take off their shoes
This sweat plodding feet
uneasy palms A second life
Sài Gòn oven of gypsy pickpockets
rasping city of neon births

Women shovel dusk into bins scrape of metal snap
of elbows Orange muffles the grunts

Sounds of the market expire
like the last chicken or catfish
men & women bargaining sun's iridescence in minor key
Woosy karaoke floods night

Eyes of flickering geodes
plum lips color of her heart Talking to me between prayer
she tells me to drink the coconut juice
eat the sliced mango take my bath
Her body lies there hearing me respond

3

Tonight a dog barks laps its breath
Whispers amplified Rice stalks marching on field of a dream

The water's edge cuts her hands legs
Gloves of suds pull
her crickets calcified in her spine
She squats so long she becomes stone
body between knees a circus act
hands apart from mind
Kneading the clothes
she rinses the water runs clear

4

The squatting toilet is a gaping mouth
The bathroom   also a kitchen washroom
has clothes hanging
like used body parts
newspaper scraps for wiping
stale clothes soaked in tubs of water
There's the quaking moment when she slips
into the hole   The slippery porcelain
with one motion swallows
her gourd hips
Her Laotian arms claw a cry down the black walls
kitchen smoking moth wings

They do all they can
to hold together her hip bones
sped to the hospital on a cyclo
Shadows run over the jostling seat
hard calves of the driver   bike wheels

5

On New Year's Eve the altar: a grapefruit and watermelon
mangoes next to mandarins
a teacup of water for thirsty spirits
dish of pork rolls   candles &
incense burning   chopsticks set on bowls of white rice

Before faded photos you pray
beg the spirits to feast

I open the book of truths:
He goes from one mistress' house
to another like opening jars of tea
wives taken on   wives seventeen children abandoned

6

She never leaves
her home in *Quận* 10 since the accident
Memories accrued in her chitin
limbs of giving birth seven times
meals cooked
for the armies
times she wanted to drown
ice herself
swim in lava climb out of her skin
pluck each eyelash

Dailiness prevents these wreckages
the grandchild's chortling
fire under kettle

7

After the monsoon quirk of weather & time people pour onto pavements He crosses the border a lizard dashes down the pagoda walls a falling star

8

The instants needles
dog tongues of water lapping my hand
I wash the clothes that fall
on their backs
My son knows where all the bars
are where the ocean
is He brings home his drink
sand his clothes

Laundry is glorious
water rises as I pour
water flushes away as I will
though the spinal cord is weak

Night rounds to a whisper
I shift from one contorted position
to another kneading the clothes
as if time won't ever
stop as if the gossip will never stop
Fungus gropes my daughter-in-law's legs
My son sets his hand on my back

9

Wanting to lose my self
the dusty streets I walk
past the convoluted mumblings of an alcoholic
past the pedicab drivers the card players
the wandering boys
advertising their vermicelli soup
past the smoky karaoke joints
the late-night eateries prowling cats
cake-faced prostitutes
posing on corner

the outline of things does not form you
a grainy strangeness takes
& I in the crowds
cross the street

This volume is the twenty-sixth
recipient of the Juniper Prize
presented annually by the
University of Massachusetts Press
for a volume of original poetry.
The prize is named in honor of
Robert Francis (1901–87), who lived
for many years at Fort Juniper,
Amherst, Massachusetts.